THE TREASURE OF INTELLIGENCE

OrangeBooks Publication

Vishwavidyalaya Marg, Civil Lines, Delhi NCR - 110054

Smriti Nagar, Bhilai, Chhattisgarh - 490020

Website: **www.orangebooks.in**

First Edition, 2019

ISBN: 978-81-944338-6-6

Price: Rs.350.00

The opinions/ contents expressed in this book are solely of the authors and do not represent the opinions/ standings/ thoughts of OrangeBooks or the Editors .

Printed in India

THE TREASURE OF INTELLIGENCE

BY

SASWATI BAG

OrangeBooks Publication

www.orangebooks.in

This book is dedicated to my son
Navoneel who forced me to learn
to frame stories.

PREFACE

I had never been into writing before. I had been a faculty of Electronics & Communication Engineering for ten years until I had no other option but to resign from my job to bring up my son. My son was always very demanding when it came to hearing stories. A time came when most story books available in the market, even everyday newspapers, magazines, science articles fell short. At last black holes, nebulas, various science experiments were included in the list of stories. Finally he suggested me to start writing stories and brought me a pen and copy. And thus I started and ended up with this edition.

Last and not the least, I would like to thank my husband Dr. Amrit Ghosh for being a constant support in this endeavour.

Haldia, West Bengal

29 October 2019   **SASWATI BAG**

CONTENTS

CH 1 : WE PLAN AND SET OFF

It was Durga Puja Holidays. My grandparents had come to our place. All of a sudden we decided to go my grandmother's birth place. I and my mother have never been to any village before. My father last went there almost twenty five years ago. It is a remote village in West Bengal. Though with time there has been a lot of development in villages, but still we were very excited. We did a very quick packing and decided to leave the day after Dussehra. We had four to five days in hand since my father's leave was ending just after Lakshmi Puja.

We were six in total - me, my parents, my grandparents and our driver uncle. We got up early and we drove off in our Scorpio by eight in the morning. There was nothing significant on our way except the changing landscape. As we left the city, the landscape gradually turned greener and greener. On the way we stopped once for tea and snacks and for quite some time, my grandmother told us about the people and place where we were going.

My grandmother's grandfather had been a very able zamindar of the place. Through agriculture, fishery and agro- based business he had made quite a lot of property. He made a palatial building that still stands as a landmark of the area. People say he even had a treasure but nobody have seen it. His son, i.e. my grandmother's father was not at all good at managing the estates. More so because he had joined the Swadeshi Movement i.e. India's struggle for independence to fight against the British. It was during this time most of the wealth was drained out, excepting a few bighas of land for agriculture and the palatial building. That was the reason why my grandmother's grandfather had hid the special treasure somewhere which nobody has found till now. Only there goes a saying "One who has the treasure of intelligence will find the real treasure".

Due to lack of money and time, the palatial building could not be maintained and it looks somewhat ghostly now- a-days. The only members staying there are my grandmother's mother, one brother and his wife. So only two rooms are enough for them. Their son stays abroad and daughter is married off. There are two more people staying there - one looks after the estate and agriculture and the other helps in cooking and looking after the house. These two persons stay in the two more rooms. Two other rooms are cleaned and used whenever somebody like us goes there. So out of 20 rooms in the house, 10 rooms on the ground floor and 10 rooms on the first floor, only 6 rooms on the ground floor are used. Rest rooms have been under lock and key for almost 15 years. So one can imagine why part of the house specially the first floor has turned ghostly. Above all, there is a very big terrace where there can be a cricket or football match easily. But with only three elderly persons at home, no one needs to go up, neither has the capacity to maintain the first floor and the terrace. There are two big ponds, one in the front and other at the back. As my grandmother said, I would see farming, fishes in the pond, hens, ducks, cows, a big flower and fruit garden once I reach there. As I kept on listening, I was just boiling with excitement. But who knew what was really in store for us for the next few days.

CH 2 : WE REACH

Around 1 pm, we reached our destination. I just could not believe my eyes. There stood a magnificent building in front of me. I was just surprised looking at the six giant pillars in front of the building. The white building still stood with its pride though at many places, black and greenish patches and banyan and peepal trees peeping here and there spoke of its age. I felt as if it was waiting for countless days to tell us all its unknown, unseen and unheard history. Our Scorpio stopped right in front of the giant staircase. As we got down, I was amazed to see the wonderful garden all around. Though it was clear that it was not taken care of properly now-a -days and was full of wild weeds, but the wild smell of some known and some unknown flowers and ripe fruits made me feel like heaven. There was a dried up marble fountain in front and huge pond at the side of the garden.

The pond had a nice sitting area in front and lined by innumerable coconut and palm trees all around. Though the sitting area of the pond was somewhat broken, the steps going down to the pond were well maintained. So my grandmother suggested that we wash our legs in the pond before we enter the house. That was really fascinating for us! My father held me tightly by one hand and my mother by his other hand. It was really refreshing dipping our legs in the cool water. I was more excited when I saw some fishes swimming up to the steps and nibbling at the weeds as we washed our legs. As we came up and sat in the shade of the coconut trees in the sitting area of the pond, I really jumped up seeing two ripe coconuts fall in the water of the pond. My father told me that the servant would swim and collect them.

CH 3 : A WARM WELCOME

By that time, my grandmother's brother had already come out to greet us. I felt like a king as we climbed up the majestic steps and entered the hall which now served the purpose of drawing and dining room. We were served homemade delicious lassi in white marble stone glasses and it was quite heavy. It was the best lassi that I have ever drunk. We met my grandmother's mother, i.e. my great grandmother and the other members staying in the house. My great grandmother was ninety seven. She was very fair. Her skin was all wrinkled. Her hair was all white and cut very short. She wore an all white saree like widows used to wear. She wore small gold stud earrings and had two gold bangles in her hands. She sat on an arm-chair and greeted us. She had a long stick standing by her chair. Probably she used it while walking. Among her wrinkled face, her bright eyes and sharp nose were very prominent.

An adjoining room was cleaned and arranged for us. Our driver uncle went to stay with the manager of the estate. It was really palatial staying here. The room was huge. One side of the room was sitting area and other side was the sleeping area. All the furniture were made of teak wood all from our own estate. The windows were huge, extending right from the floor to the ceiling. One can have a wonderful view of the garden through the windows. The fans hung from the ceiling with long rods. We were told there was often power cuts or low voltages. So candles and matchsticks were kept. In the sleeping area, in one corner there was a king size teakwood bed where my parents would sleep and in the other corner there was a medium size bed for me to sleep. Mosquito nets were kept with each bed. There was an attached bathroom which was also huge. But it was renovated with modern facilities with time. After we refreshed ourselves, we had our lunch. It was a traditional Bengali lunch in brass utensils. After lunch, we went to take rest. My parents kept on talking with each other while I roamed about looking all around the room, outside through the windows until I felt sleepy. Usually on school days, I rarely get a chance to sleep during the day. So I didn't want to lose the chance of sleeping today and went off to sleep.

CH 4 : DAY 1 : WE ENJOY NATURE

When I woke up, the sunshine was almost gone. In fact my mother called me up. After tea and delicious homemade coconut laddoos, we decided to have a look within the boundary itself. The garden was really magnificent with mango, jackfruit, blackberry, chikoo, star fruit, custard apple, rose berry, water apple, jujubes, lemons of varied types, litchis, banana and the list goes on. There were also several varieties of hibiscuses, roses, yellow oleander, pink oleander, golden shower, gulmohar, bougainvillea, gardenia, champak, periwinkle, tube rose, varieties of jasmines and many more. The boundary walls were lined by teak, sal and betel nut trees. There were also neem and basil all around. My grandfather taught me to recognize so many plants.

The backyard had a few more mango trees, few tamarind trees. There was also a cow shed with two cows, a number of cocks, hens and ducks kept in large cage areas. There was also a small pond in the backyard. I felt as if I was in a botanical garden. My father had already told the servant to clean the stairs and part of the terrace.

As we went up the big steps of the terrace, we could still feel the stuffy smell all around. The terrace was like a mini football ground. As it was darkening, the full moon started rising through the swaying leaves of the coconut trees. I felt as if I had reached a completely different part of the earth. There was sound of conch shells one after another. Mother said people were offering evening puja and I also saw my grandmother placing a diya in front of the holy basil plant in the garden down.

CH 5: AN EERIE NIGHT

After an early dinner, we went to bed. Night seems to get deeper so early in villages. As my father switched off the light, I felt a little weird. Only a dim bulb was glowing outside the entrance of our room. As I started to feel sleepy, suddenly there was power cut. I got frightened and called my father.My father had kept a torch near his head while sleeping. He switched it on and went to the windows to move the curtains. Shining moonlight came into the room with a fresh cool breeze. It created a romantic atmosphere but I felt as if something shadowy was there. The smell of the night flowers filled the atmosphere all around.A cat mewed somewhere and I felt so eerie, I ran to my father and decided to sleep with him that night. With my father in between, mother on the other side, I slept and held my father's hand tightly. Somewhere in the garden, a nocturnal bird screamed. There was a chorus of insects all around. Far away a fox howled. Several fire flies had entered the room. I saw them shining their tiny torches to find their ways in the dark. I had never been in such an uncomfortable environment before. To overcome my fright, I started thinking of Tom & Jerry and really didn't realize when I fell asleep.

CH 6 : DAY 2 BEGINS JOYFULLY

Next day morning, my mother woke me up a bit early to show me the milking of cows. As I opened my eyes, I was so delighted at the sight of the garden outside filled with colorful flowers. Birds were chirping all around. The atmosphere was so different from that of the previous night. I got up quickly, and got ready to see milking of cows. It was fun collecting the eggs of the hens and ducks. I learnt to differentiate between the eggs of hens and ducks. The duck egg is smoother and whiter than that of a hen. Next we went to see fishing using big fishing nets in our pond. Two men from the village were called for fishing. As the men pulled up the fishing nets, I was also jumping like the jumping fishes. A few were taken for cooking and the smaller ones were again released in the water. By the time we came home and took bath, it was almost lunch time.

After lunch, again I had a good sleep. I got up and as the heat outside started to reduce we got ready to explore the nearby places. It was really fun walking along the narrow paths between the fields. On one side, the field was filled with variety of green vegetables and on the other side, the paddy plants swayed in the gentle breeze. Still some people were working in their fields. I was amused to see real scarecrows. My grandfather talked to some of the villagers. Some people were returning homes with their cows and goats. Life here was so different. There was no hustle bustle of the city. It was so serene all around. As darkness began to spread its wings, birds started returning to their nests. The almost full moon began to rise up from the horizon. In cities, we never get to see a horizon; the skyline has only big buildings. As the moon began to rise high above our heads, we sat by a canal side watching the gleaming moonlight flood the pasture all around. Water lilies stared to bloom in the canal water and the white water lilies shining in the moonlight seemed to take us to heaven. It was quite late and we decided to return home.

It was low voltage. Only dim bulbs were glowing in the house. That created a more ghostly atmosphere. I felt shadows moving here and there. We, all family members, finally settled in the drawing room with tea, samosas and alu tikkis. It was so tasty. In fact food had to be tasty as vegetables, milk, fish, chicken, fruits, eggs everything were all farm- fresh. I asked my great grandmother to tell me stories.

CH 7 : STORY TIME

She began with clearing her throat. The initial things she said was already known to me from my grandmother. She added that her father-in-law, i.e. my grandmother's grandfather was a very sophisticated person. He was much ahead of his time in his thoughts and actions. He was an avid reader. He used to buy a lot of books from Kolkata. He even used to collect English novels. He was even good in writing. He wrote poems and rhymes both in Bengali and English. He was an excellent football player. Once in a year, he brought in teams from various places and arranged football tournaments. He even himself played in the tournament wearing khaki half pant and shirt. He even had a mini zoo with various animals and birds behind the house. Before he died, he set all the animals free. He brought in artists from Kolkata to draw portraits. He had a group of well trained wrestlers who were also apt in sword fighting, hunting with spears etc.

Then great grandmother told me how dacoits used to came to loot the houses in those days. The dacoit leader used to send a letter mentioning when they'll be coming to attack. They used to walk on two long bamboo sticks to walk at incredible speed and rubbed excess mustard oil on their bodies which helped them to escape easily if somehow caught them by chance. She told me incidents of how dacoits were resisted in our house.

Then she told about her husband, i.e. my great grandfather. She told how his husband got involved in Swadeshi Movement, how the

Swadeshis i.e. the freedom fighters used to hide in our house, how the British came to ransack our house, how charkhas i.e. spinning wheels came in. In fact she herself had also worked on charkhas. It was really interesting to hear the old stories.

Then I asked her about the treasure of this house. She told that when she came in here as a very young bride, she had seen pots of gold and silver coins. There were lots of antique jewelleries. At that time a heavy gold necklace costed just Rs. 100! But everything drained out with time. But the will or testament left behind by her father- in -law has a line at the end "One who has the treasure of intelligence will get my real treasure." I leaped up in excitement! I had heard this before! So, there was really treasure somewhere here!! I asked great grandmother if there were any antique things left behind somewhere in the house. I would like to see those. She said that there were a lot of such things kept in the "Naachghar" which was a big hall in one side of the ground floor where all musical programmes used to be held on special occasions. But the room hasn't been opened for ages. So we would have to break open the door.

It was already dinner time. We did not realize how time flied out. After dinner we planned that the next day's mission would be to explore the Naachghar before bath as it would be extremely dusty and dirty all around. I went to sleep with my parents, though I was almost accustomed to the environment by then. I felt too much excited for the next day.

CH 8 : DAY 3 : LET'S EXPLORE

Next day after breakfast, we prepared ourselves for the exploration. We made our team - me, my parents, my grandfather and our driver uncle. We first tied our heads with clothes like scarves and wore dust masks also. Luckily my mother had brought some dust masks in case the village roads were dusty. We all wore full sleeve clothes and covered shoes and full pants. My father gathered a hammer, a big torch and broke a few long branches from the trees in the garden. I really felt we were working on a mission. We all gathered in front of the Naachghar's huge door. The lock was really heavy and big and was totally rusted. My father began hitting it hard by the hammer. Though it was rusted, my father had to hit it several times to break it open. Now it was time to push open the door. I was excited but tensed. Would a lot of bats fly out? Or would there be snakes wriggling inside? Would a pack of rats chase me? How big would be the spiders inside? Really I was getting afraid. My father and driver uncle started pushing the door with all their strength.

After several pushes, the door finally opened making scary sounds. It was so dark inside. We felt a severe dusty smell. The air inside was really suffocating. My father switched on the torch. As the strong beam of the light shone through the room, I really trembled in fear. There were big cobwebs everywhere. My father told us to wait outside. He and our driver uncle entered first with the big branches of trees. As they entered, they made their way by destroying the cobwebs with the branches and the first thing they did was to force open all the huge windows of the room. As we waited outside, I could hear my own palpitation. We could hear how the persons inside were hitting each window to force open them. As one by one window was opened, sunlight spread inside. Me, my mother and my grandfather then entered slowly. There was such a peculiar smell inside. Luckily there were no bats, rats or snakes. Only spiders and cockroaches were running everywhere. I felt so creepy. The next thing my father and driver uncle did was to remove the white bed sheets that covered each and every furniture in the room with the long branches. All the covering sheets were then dumped in one empty corner of the room. After all the sheets and cobwebs were removed, the room looked somewhat comfortable.

I could see three huge spears hanging at a place on the wall. There were also two big guns and six swords and shields. The furniture which were dumped in that room were also antique, all made of teakwood and had beautiful carvings. My mother sighed if she could have space to keep those beds, book cases, dressing tables, centre tables, lamp stands in our flat. As I looked up, I could see a huge chandelier hanging from the ceiling at the centre of the room. My father collected a long rod from a place in the room and used it to remove the huge cloth that covered the chandelier. As the cloth fell, there was in fact a dust storm. Luckily we had our dust masks on. As we looked up, there hang a fascinating piece of artwork - a chandelier made of brass. I just imagined how gorgeous it would have looked when all the candles of the chandelier glowed together in the dark evenings. All electric lights today are merely nothing compared to the glow that this chandelier created.

On the other wall of the room, we could see the stuffed heads of deer, antelopes and even that of a tiger showing its teeth, all faded after such a long time. Now the air was much fresh as more and more fresh air entered through the huge windows. We started exploring the room now. But the book cases, dressing tables were all empty. I had longed to find a clue for the treasure here. So I started feeling sad, when I suddenly noticed a big iron trunk box kept under the bed.

As I shouted in excitement as if all the treasure was kept inside that trunk, my father and driver uncle really struggled hard to pull out the trunk. It was really heavy and had a huge lock. Again my father broke the lock with the hammer. As he lifted the heavy lid of the trunk, to my dismay, I found lots and lots of thick books kept inside. My father began to take out the books one by one. As he piled them on the bed, we saw there were Bengali novels of eminent writers, a lot of Bengali short story collections, Bengali poem collections and travel stories. Even there were a few English Novels and English poem collections. Each book was really precious, all with velvet covers and names written in golden alphabets. How gorgeous these books were compared to the paper backs we get today! Really my great great grandfather was an avid reader. At the extreme bottom, my father found three diaries with leather covers. My father stared at my mother for a moment and handed over the three diaries to her. Did he expect to get something special in those diaries? I tried to read my father's face. My grandfather then told to leave everything in that room in that uncovered condition so that the dusty awkward smell could fade within the next few days and later we could have a discussion and decide what could be done with those antique pieces. I wished if I could bring my friends to show them all these.

32

CH 9 : LET'S SOLVE THE RIDDLES

We all went back to the drawing room and narrated all that happened to the rest of the family members. We then went back to our respective rooms, took bath and ultimately I felt fresh like never before. All our dusty clothes were sent to be washed properly. We then had our grand traditional lunch as we were having each day and went to have rest. As I lay down on my bed and looked outside at the magnificent garden, my father opened and kept the diaries on one place of the floor where there was strong sunlight. He said if he did not do that we all would severely sneeze while going through the diaries. After a short nap and a brisk walk, we had the evening tea and snacks. I could not wait any longer and we all came to our room. Now we started going through the diaries together. The first diary had an expensive leather cover. All the entries were made in green ink. All the entries were Bengali poems - may be written by the great zamindar, my great great grandfather or collected by him. Now we began browsing through the second diary. This also had an expensive leather cover. Here also all the entries were made in green ink. But this diary had all English poems and some travel experiences written in English. Really the zamindar was an educated person ahead of his time. Now it was the turn for the last diary. This also had the same leather cover. Here also the entries were in green ink. As we read through, we found riddles, rhymes both in English and Bengali. There were some calculations, may be regarding the expenses of the house, or debit-credit of the estate. There were also some personal entries. This diary had miscellaneous topics entered in it. But we suddenly noticed something - a few pages in between had entry in red ink! We three looked at each other. Was it something special? By that time, I heard my grandmother call us for dinner. We decided to go through the red ink entries as we return immediately after dinner.

We rushed back to our room after dinner. My mother quickly made the beds. My father closed the door and we three sat together inside the mosquito net. My father started reading the portion written in red ink slowly:

Its body extends,

Long and wide.

Run along it,

Drive or ride

On a horse,

Or in a car,

It's upon you to decide

You'll go how far.

It begins

Just where it ends,

And your palatial house

There stands.

....

How many legs has a bee?

How many legs has a spider?

I have 4 bees in a box

And 4 spiders in another.

There are three squirrels on the tree

And three birds sing in the cages.

Can you tell how many legs

They altogether have?

....

The petals of this flower

Danced in the wind,

When I went to pluck it,

It quickly took wing.

....

Has no limbs

Kept only for fun

It is round

And constantly on the run.

....

It is blue,

And green,

And brown.

It shows rivers, mountains,

Countries, cities,

And seas –

All are there

For us to see.

....

It wakes us up

Every day,

Whether the sky is

Clear or grey,

We open our eyes,

Stretch and rise

Once it rises

In the skies.

....

He makes nets -

But doesn't fish!

Neither related to mosquitoes

If you can't think

You're a foolish!

....

It is running

Night and day,

But it can never

Run away.

....

It has four legs

Either straight or bent

But it cannot walk

Needs a lot of them in any event.

....

This was really puzzling. What was this - just some random riddles or some important clue to the treasure? We all looked at each other. My father told very seriously in a low voice that we had only the next day in hand. The day after tomorrow was Lakshmi Puja and during Puja at home when some neighbours will come, it'll be impossible to carry out investigations. After that his leave was ending, so we have to go back at any cost. So we had only one night to find out if really the red inked portion had any meaning.

So my mother read the first riddle a bit loudly. It has a long and wide body .... can run, drive or ride on horse or car .... it begins at our house.... it ends at our house .... it's the road that ended in our house .... does it mean the treasure is in the house itself?

I was getting excited. Now the next riddle .... what type of riddle is this?.... bee, spider, squirrel, bird ... does it have anything to with zamindar's mini zoo? Let's solve the sum. Each bee has 6 legs, Total 4 x 6 = 24 legs. Each spider has 8 legs. Total 4 x 8 = 32 legs. Each squirrel has 4 legs. Total 3 x 4 = 12 legs. Each bird has 2 legs. Total 3 x 2 = 6 legs. So grand total of 74 legs. What to do with 74 legs? Father cried out is it indicating to 74 steps? But where to measure 74 steps? Road to the zoo? Or inside the house? But first riddle indicates the road ending and the house starting. So should we measure the footsteps from the entrance gate? It was really confusing. Mother told that tomorrow morning father should try measuring the footsteps and see where it leads. As I was a teenager and mother a woman, so the footsteps of zamindar, if we are predicting in the right path, would surely be comparable to my father's. So we had no option than to wait till next morning.

Now the third riddle .... flower petals with wings .... I cried out .... it's surely a butterfly!

Now the fourth riddle .... no legs .... round .... run .... fun .... it's a ball.

Now the fifth puzzle .... shows rivers, mountains, countries, cities.... blue seas, green plains, brown mountains .... yes! ... a map...Father said that it could be a globe also!

The next riddle was easy .... we quickly made out it was the Sun.

Now the seventh riddle .... nets .... mosquito net ? fishing net ? but not fishing .... neither mosquito makes net .... then what? mother cried .... spider making net .... cobweb?

The second last riddle .... what is running day and night .... time?....clock!!

And the last riddle .... four legs .... cannot walk .... legs straight or bent.... that was quite easy .... a chair!!

So father summed up on a piece of paper ....

1. road/ house
2. 74 steps / zoo / house
3. flower / butterfly
4. ball / football
5. map/ globe
6. sun
7. spider / cobweb

8. time/ clock

9. chair

We really didn't know how time ran out. It was already past three in the morning. My father said that we should immediately go to sleep as the next morning was very vital. I was too excited to go to sleep. After turning sides for a number of time, I really didn't know when I felt asleep.

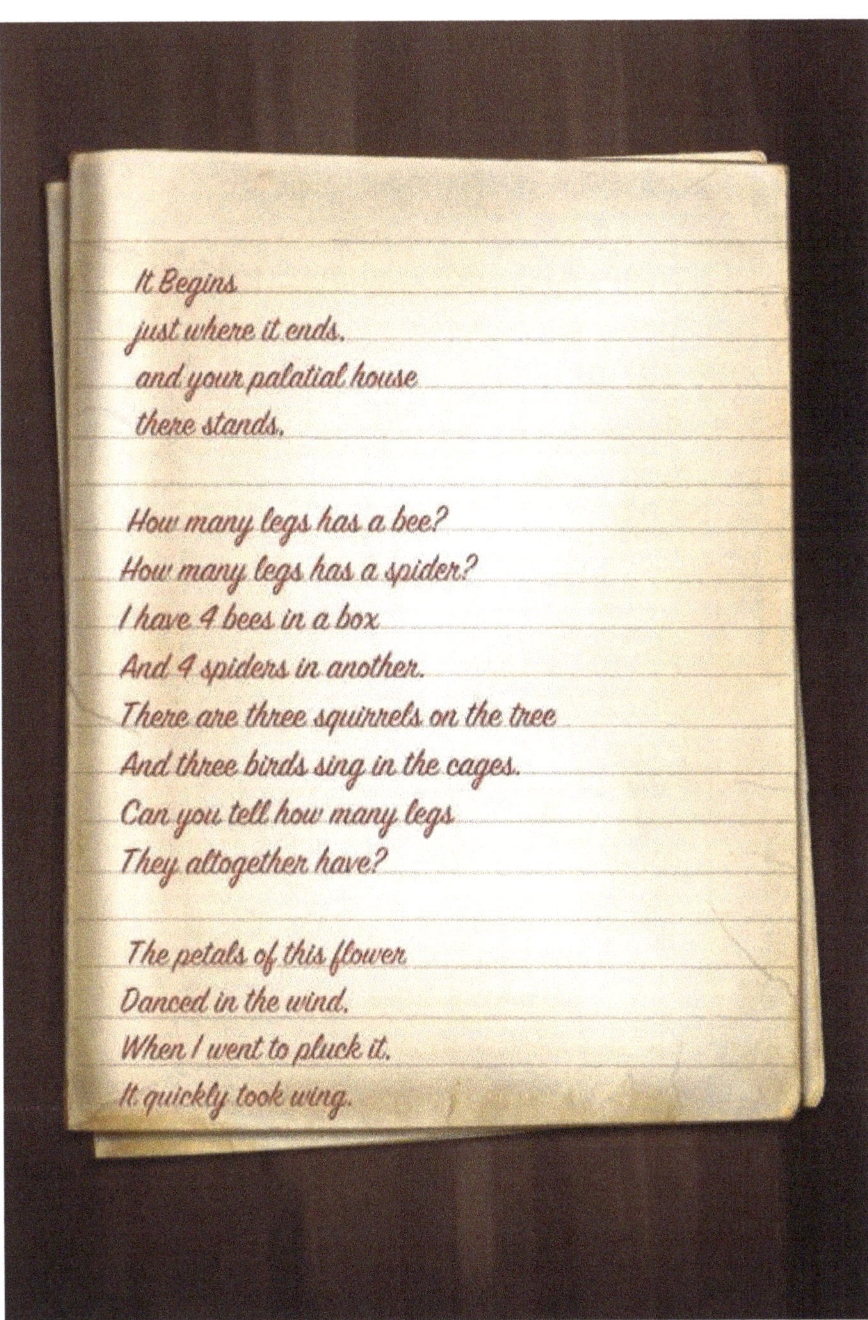

It Begins
just where it ends,
and your palatial house
there stands,

How many legs has a bee?
How many legs has a spider?
I have 4 bees in a box
And 4 spiders in another.
There are three squirrels on the tree
And three birds sing in the cages.
Can you tell how many legs
They altogether have?

The petals of this flower
Danced in the wind.
When I went to pluck it,
It quickly took wing.

CH 10 : TIME TO FIND THE TREASURE

I was going through a dark cave. Bats were hanging from the ceiling. Some bats were flying out of the cave. From somewhere I could hear the sound of a stream. My torch was growing dimmer and dimmer. Suddenly a snake stood in front of me with open hood. I was sweating in fear when I suddenly jumped up. My mother was calling me to get up. I was so much occupied with the thoughts of treasure that I was dreaming I went to a treasure hunt in a cave.

I got ready quickly and went for breakfast. Then my parents and I stood at the entrance door of the house. We were determined to find out if at all the riddles had any meaning. My mother told that measuring 74 steps outside the house and finding out any probable spot was just like finding a needle in a hay stock. So my father started walking 74 steps from the entrance door into the house on the ground floor. But to our disappointment, he stopped at a place on the verandah which had apparently nothing significant all around. So we decided that we should go upstairs while measuring the steps. Again father started from the entrance door, but this time he walked towards the stairs and started going up. This time, the place where he stopped on the first floor was just in front of a door of a large room. We were excited. We needed to explore this room.

We ran downstairs and called everybody to the drawing room. Everybody was told about the developments since last night. Everybody looked at each other in excitement. My grandmother's brother told that since this was a sensitive issue it was better that all family members would be present while we carry on our investigations. And as per our plan, father sent our driver, manager and servant of the house to get all the things for Lakshmi Puja tomorrow. The list was long, and the big market was quite far off. So it would be almost three hours before they returned. As we heard the sound of the car fading away, the main door was locked.

We all geared up like the previous day of exploration. In addition, my father gathered big screwdriver, pliers, knife, a pair of scissors, rope, chisel and pieces of old clothes for wiping. We planned we would take great grandmother later on after we make the room somewhat comfortable. Just like the previous day of exploration, the lock was broken, all the big windows were forced open, the cobwebs were destroyed with the big branches and lastly all the covering sheets were removed and gathered at a place on the verandah. My grandmother's brother and my grandfather carried great grandmother upstairs and she was made to sit on a chair.

We first looked around and closely observed the room. Great grandmother said that room belonged to that zamindar, my great great grandfather. The room was very large. There was a sleeping area which had a king size delicately curved teakwood bed.

Beside that, was the dressing area. There was a beautiful dressing table, a huge almirah at the corner of the room and arrangement for hanging clothes.

On the other side of the room was the sitting area which had couches and a centre table.

On one side of the sitting area was the study area. There was a teakwood reading table and a chair. Beside that was a book case which still had several books.

Besides that, there was a small corner of worship as there stood a beautiful statue of Lord Krishna.

As usual there was a beautiful candle chandelier hanging from the centre of the room, though this was not huge like the previous one. Also, there were two large portraits of the zamindar hanging on the wall of the room.

Now we started looking for clues all around. My father had the piece of paper on which last night he had written down the probable clues. Suddenly I noticed, in one of the portraits, the zamindar standing in a gorgeous dress. Beside him, there was an intrically carved wooden stool with a flower vase on it. The roses in the vase were unusually big and had much brighter color than the rest of the picture. I told everybody, and my father brought in a tall stool kept in the stairways. He climbed up and we held by the sides. It was really difficult to bring down such a big portrait. Suddenly an idea struck to me. I told my father to cut open the backside of the portrait. Using the scissors and the knife, he started cutting the back layers of the huge picture frame. As he started removing the layers and sunlight fell over it through the window, suddenly there was a dazzle. We looked with wide open eyes as father brought out a dazzling butterfly brooch studded with multicolored precious stones. Eureka! We were on right path! Everybody was now super excited.

The next clue was easily found out. There was another portrait where the zamindar was wearing the outfit of a sportsman, holding a trophy in his hand, and a football lay near his feet. We had heard that he was a great football enthusiast. We again brought down this portrait and my father started cutting this one also. We all bent over and looked to see what came out this time. My goodness! It was a huge gold necklace with red rubies and green emeralds. I wondered how on earth anyone could wear such a heavy and big necklace! But this was a real treasure!

The next clue was easily identified. There was a globe on the reading table. But what to do with the globe? My father removed the globe from its stand and shook it hard. There was something shaking inside it. My father tried to find out any probable joint on the globe. He tore up the map over the wooden globe, and then with the chisel forced opened the joint of the wooden hemisphere. Ultimately, it broke off, and almost 20 silver coins dropped down! Everyone in the room became almost numb. There was pin-drop silence! I wondered what else was in store for us.

Our next clue was sun. We all looked around, but there was no sign of any sun. It was so puzzling! Suddenly my mother cried out.

Earlier days, it was normal for people to take bath in the pond. Many of them performed Surya Pranam after taking bath. So sun must be related to worship. And in the room, there was …. Lord Krishna! We all rushed to the corner, only great grandmother kept sitting on her chair and watched. Lord Krishna was placed on a wooden shelf. My father tried to pull the statue several times, but in vain. Then he tried to give it a twist. After several tries, he felt the statue might have moved a little. So this time, I joined hands with him and we together tried to twist the statue. At last! The statue moved and came out. There was quite a big hollow in the wooden base! Mother warned us first to check the hollow with torchlight; it was quite unsafe to put our hands inside. My father shone his torchlight in the hollow and brought out a statue of Lord Ganesha about 10 inches height made of white stone. Then again he brought out a similar statue of Goddess Lakshmi made of white stone. Though the carvings were very intricate, but why would someone hide marble statues in this way? My father kept peeping inside. I asked was there anything more? My father again put his hands inside and brought out an intricately curved white stone jewellery box. We all crowded over him as he opened the box. There were a comb and a pen made of the same material. I said aloud, why would anyone make comb and pen out of white marble and hide it this way? After a brief pause, my grandmother cried out that those were not made of white marble, but that material was ivory! What! Ivory, that means elephant tusk! The Ganesha - Lakshmi idols, the jewellery box, the comb and the pen were all made of ivory! Now it was really getting hard to digest everything! I felt as if I had reached King Solomon's mines!

Time was running out!! Any time driver uncle could return back. Before they returned, we needed to complete our mission. By now, father was really tired but he carried on without wasting any time. Our next clue was spider / cobweb. This time again, mother said, spiders are generally found behind furniture. So should we concentrate behind the almirah! That huge heavy almirah! How could we remove that! This time along with my father, I, my mother, my grandfather and my grandmother's brother all joined hands together and pushed the almirah to one side. What to do next? I saw father tapping the walls with his hands. Suddenly at one point, the sound changed. My father tapped and tapped that portion of the wall and said that the portion was hollow. So what was inside! As my father began to break the wall with the heavy hammer, I feared if there would be snakes inside! My father told that there would be probably no source of oxygen inside; in any case no snake would survive. It really was very hard to break open the wall. At last! There appeared the opening of a cave inside! Mother laughed and said it could be only a hidden shelf and not a cave. Father shone the torchlight and brought out an earthen pot whose month was covered by a red cloth which had turned pale after ages. As father removed the red cloth, our hearts seemed to stop beating. Gold coins! Almost 50 coins as my father counted!

Last two clues were left and very little time in hand. What else could be found! I could not imagine anything more .... We already got a precious stone studded gold butterfly brooch, heavy gold necklace with rubies and emeralds, 20 silver coins, Lord Ganesha and Goddess Lakshmi statues, jewellery box, comb and pen all made from ivory and 50 gold coins. What more could we expect!!

Our next clue was watch. Near the sitting area, there was a big grandfather's clock which had stopped long ago. My father bought it down very carefully. I told if the pendulum was made of gold. But my father said that it was unlikely as he used his screwdriver to open the back case of the big clock. And we got it! There was a gold pocket watch with a gold chain with tiny diamonds shining all along the rim of the watch!

And the last clue was chair. We all rushed to the reading area. My father ripped open the leather seat of the chair with his knife. But nothing was there! So where do we look for the last treasure? Father instantly turned the chair upside down. I suddenly noticed that there were rubber pieces attached at the bottom of the legs of the chair. Three of the rubber pieces were round while the last one was square. Why? As I told father about my observation, he began to pull the square rubber piece with the pliers and chisel. Suddenly the rubber piece came out and big white pearls each of the size of a marble rolled out on the floor. This was really more than enough! We collected almost 20 pearls.

CH 11 : WE MADE IT!

We quickly packed all the treasure in a big bag. By the time we all came down, we heard the sound of the car stopping at the doorsteps. Thank God! We were just in time! We were all extremely tired by now. We all went to our rooms to get clean and fresh! My grandfather carried the treasure bag to his room. We met at dinner. The dinner table was unusually silent. Everybody completed their dinner without uttering a single word. After dinner, when all the servants went back to their rooms, we all met in great grandmother's room. The door was closed and great grandmother said that as per the will of her father- in-law, the treasure will go to three of us - me and my parents. We were just awestruck with excitement!

Next morning, preparations started for Lakshmi Puja. I helped my mother with the Alpona in front of the Goddess. Alpona is the form of Rangoli practiced in Bengal. In the afternoon our packing was almost completed. My mother and grandmother were very much tensed regarding how we could take so much treasure with us for such a long journey. It was decided that part of the treasure would be kept in grandmother's locker while the rest would be kept in my mother's locker. Later at some time, all the relatives and family members would be called in together to decide whether the place could be renovated to make a heritage tourist place. In the evening several neighbours came to our place during the puja. After all the puja rituals were complete, we had our dinner. Then we decide to sit in the sitting area of the pond for quite some time to enjoy the flooding moon light. On one hand, I felt sad to leave the place, the beauty of nature, the warmth of the family members here, while on the other hand I longed to get back to my own home, my school, my friends. We went to bed early.

Next morning, we were almost ready and having breakfast. I saw my father gathering a lot of bags. I went up to see what it was all about. Two bags were full of vegetables from the field like pumpkin, spinach, tomatoes, striped gourds, brinjal, beans, raw mangoes and a lot more. Among fruits I saw my father had collected bananas, custard apple, guavas, chikoos, pineapple, star fruits, lemons. I really wondered why we were taking home so many fruits and vegetables. My mother said that we don't get so farm fresh fruits and vegetables in the city.

There was another bag full of eatables. As I peeped into the bag, I saw packets of coconut laddoos, sesame laddoos, puffed rice laddoos, bottles of salted flattened rice, packets of puffed rice, some varieties of homemade namkeens. There was another bag full of green and ripe coconuts. There were bottle of homemade ghee, mango pickles, dried mangoes, box of tamarind, two crates of egg carefully packed. I was really getting puzzled by then.

I lost my words when I saw a big aluminum container with quite a number of fishes swimming in water. The mouth of the container was carefully sealed with a plastic sheet to allow flow of air into the container. Father instructed driver uncle and the servant to carefully load all the bags under the seats and the container at the back of the scorpio. Along with that we had our own luggage.

I asked mother whether we'll get space to sit. Meanwhile while everybody was busy, I suddenly saw my father bring the bag of treasure and slip it under the seats in between the other bags. Now I really understood the matter. Everything was done just to hide the treasure bag within the crowd of other bags.

At last we bid goodbye to everybody. As our car started, I looked back through the window. I saw tears rolling down the cheeks of my great grandmother. I waved my hands and promised to return back very soon. I had to come back by Holi. This time I wanted to see the yellow mustard fields spreading sunshine across the horizon.

9 788194 433866